For everyone who loves and embraces human desires

NATE HALIV: PLEASE EXCUSE ME FOR NOT BEING SHAKESPEARE

This is a work of fiction. Names, characters, places, and incidents are either products of the author's imagination or, if real, are used fictitiously. All statements, activities, stunts, descriptions, information, and other materials contained herein are intended for entertainment purposes only. They should not be relied upon for accuracy or attempted or replicated; doing so may result in legal consequences.

Copyright © 2024 Nate Haliv.
For inquiries: natehaliv@gmail.com
All rights reserved. No part of this book may be reproduced, transmitted, or stored in an information retrieval system in any form or by any means, graphic, electronic, or mechanical, including photocopying, taping, and recording, without prior written permission from the author.

NATE HALIV: PLEASE EXCUSE ME FOR NOT BEING SHAKESPEARE

1. BIRTHDAY SEX

The morning sun was cutting through the blind,
My seventeenth birthday, the day was undefined.
Then Pamela came knocking at my door,
Across the hall, stepping on my floor.

She wore a simple shirt, oversized and white,
But nothing underneath to hide the sight.
Her nipples pressed against the cotton thin,
She looked me up and down with a devil's grin.

"Happy birthday," she whispered, voice so low,
"I didn't wrap a gift, I hope you know."
She grabbed my wrist, her grip was hot and tight,
And pulled me to her room, out of the light.

I watched her walk, the heavy, rhythmic sway,
Her ass cheeks moving in a hypnotic way.
"Sit down," she said, and pointed to the bed,
A thousand dirty thoughts rushed through my head.

I sat there frozen, waiting for the cue,
She stepped between my knees to get a view.
The metal of my belt gave a heavy clink,
She pulled the zipper down before I could blink.

She freed me into the air, hard and ready,
Her breathing getting deep and unready.
"You ready to go to heaven?" she asked me then,
Looking like the wildest kind of sin.

I nodded fast, my throat too dry to speak,

NATE HALIV: PLEASE EXCUSE ME FOR NOT BEING SHAKESPEARE

She dropped down low, making my knees go weak.
She took me in her mouth, so wet and warm,
A sudden, violent, perfect kind of storm.

She sucked the soul right out from underneath,
With nothing but her lips, no sign of teeth.
"Do you want more?" she mumbled against the skin,
I gasped for air and let the room spin.

She pushed me back, "No touching," she commanded,
The bossiest demand she'd ever landed.
She stripped the shirt, her body free and bare,
With heavy breasts and messy morning hair.

She crawled up on the mattress, on all fours,
Like she was settling all our silent scores.
She hovered right above my face to tease,
"Now eat me up," she said, "and aim to please."

She tasted like a peach, distinct and sweet,
I used my tongue to make the job complete.
Her juices ran, a slick and heavy glaze,
I was lost inside a thick and lustful haze.

Her thighs clamped tight around my buzzing ears,
Erasing all my shy and awkward fears.
"Damn boy," she moaned, "you use that tongue so well,"
She shook and shivered under her own spell.

She spun around and straddled on my waist,
Moving with a desperate, hungry haste.
No condom on, just skin and raw friction,

NATE HALIV: PLEASE EXCUSE ME FOR NOT BEING SHAKESPEARE

Feeding into a brand new addiction.

We pounded hard, the sweat began to drip,
I held her hips with a bruising finger grip.
She spoke in tongues, her eyes rolled back and white,
The window filled with sharp and morning light.

"Look at me," she said, "look deep inside,"
There was nowhere left for either one to hide.
I spilled my seeds, a flood I couldn't stop,
While she collapsed right there upon the top.

She licked the evidence off, slow and clean,
The wildest movie that I'd ever seen.
"Best birthday ever?" she asked with a trace of fun,
The best indeed, before the day had begun.

2. A NIGHT WITH SARAH

You came to my door with a secret to keep,
While your boyfriend at home was likely asleep.
"I need to know," you whispered so low,
"If the rumors are true, I just have to know."

You wanted the danger, the fruit on the tree,
To see what a man of color brings to be.
I opened the door and I pulled you inside,
With nowhere for you or your demons to hide.

I peeled off your dress, watching it fall,
Pushing your back up against the white wall.

NATE HALIV: PLEASE EXCUSE ME FOR NOT BEING SHAKESPEARE

Your skin was so pale, a contrast to mine,
Like milk in the shadows, chaotic and fine.

Your nipples were hard, responding to air,
I traced down your curves with a deliberate care.
I fell to my knees to worship the view,
The red, weeping center belonging to you.

"Oh God," you gasped out, tangling your hand,
In the coils of my hair, just like we planned.
You tasted of peaches and salty desire,
My tongue was the match that lit up the fire.

You spoke in a language I didn't quite know,
German and French in a steady, hot flow.
You begged me to stop, then begged for some more,
Writhing around on the hardwood floor.

Then you pulled me up, with a look in your eye,
"Take me right now," came your desperate cry.
"My Nigerian Prince," you said in my ear,
"Make me yours," you demanded, loud and clear.

You dropped to your knees and opened your lips,
Taking me deep with a sway of your hips.
You looked up at me with that sinful, sly grin,
Happy to drown in the depth of your sin.

"Turn around," I told you, my voice like a stone,
You arched up your back, letting out a soft moan.
"Take me from behind," you pleaded again,
Seeking the pleasure and seeking the pain.

I gripped on your waist and I entered you slow,
Then picked up the pace, letting go, letting go.
Two shallow, three deep, finding the spot,
The room getting heavy and humid and hot.

You screamed out my name, forgetting his face,
Lost in the rhythm and lost in the pace.
"Faster," you yelled, "don't stop, don't you dare,"
Your fingers were clawing at nothing but air.

I felt the release start to build in my chest,
I poured myself in you and gave you my best.
We collapsed on the sheets, the sweat on our skin,
Soaking in silence and soaking in sin.

"Clean me up," I whispered, pulling away,
You did as I asked, wishing I'd stay.
But I dressed in the dark, my desire now dim,
I walked out the door and left on a whim.

3. PLEASE EXCUSE ME FOR NOT BEING SHAKESPEARE

Forgive me, Will, for I have no plays to show,
No Hamlet, no Macbeth, no literary glow.
You wrote one hundred fifty-four sonnets with a pen,
I've been inside one hundred eighty-seven women.

White, Black, Latina, I don't discriminate,
I leave my mark on them, I seal their fate.
You spent your life with ink upon the page,

NATE HALIV: PLEASE EXCUSE ME FOR NOT BEING SHAKESPEARE

I spend my nights performing on a different stage.

I can't write Romeo, or Juliet in the tomb,
I'd rather write about the sweat inside the room.
Society is scared, they hide beneath the sheet,
Terrified of pleasure, terrified of heat.

But this is my diary, the raw and dirty truth,
The things we actually do inside the dark of youth.
We crave the rush, the climax, and the sound,
But keep our wildest secrets buried underground.

I don't find inspiration in a dusty old book,
I find it in a moan, a touch, a hungry look.
I get my best ideas when a girl sits on my face,
My tongue deep inside her, winning the race.

Or watching white powder on a dark and perfect rear,
Snorting up the magic, making vision clear.
My melanin queen lets me use her skin,
To rack up a line and let the games begin.

My bibliography is short, my list is bare,
But what I pack downstairs is beyond compare.
I make them catch feelings with a simple stroke,
This isn't poetry, and this isn't a joke.

My verses won't make you weep a sad tear,
But my tongue on your woman's spot makes you shake with fear.
Screaming "Oh God" until the neighbors know,
That's the only kind of rhythm that I show.

NATE HALIV: PLEASE EXCUSE ME FOR NOT BEING SHAKESPEARE

So pardon the grammar, if the English is rough,
My second language isn't elegant enough.
My fingers fumble when they try to type a rhyme,
But put them inside her? They work every time.

I know the exact way to make the fountain start,
A different kind of skill, a different kind of art.
I don't need a quill to make a woman gush,
I just need the friction, the heat, and the rush.

So keep your iambic, and your pentameter too,
I'll stick to the threesomes and the things that we do.
I'm not a playwright, I don't wear the crown,
I'm just the guy who takes your girlfriend down.

The name is Nate Haliv, remember the text,
Not a god of drama, but a God of Sex.

4. FACETIME WITH CAMILA

I woke up hard inside the morning light
The sheet was tented up with heavy might
My body was an aching heavy wire
Consumed by blood and burning with the fire
I lay alone within the empty bed
And thoughts of need were spinning in my head

I grabbed the phone to call the Tinder date
The one with whom the hour is never late
She answered with a raspy voice and yawn
Inside the early breaking of the dawn

NATE HALIV: PLEASE EXCUSE ME FOR NOT BEING SHAKESPEARE

She told me that the voice was not enough
And that the morning time was very rough

She switched to video to see my face
She looked amazing in her sleeping space
She asked me why I woke her from her rest
I told her that I had a heavy test
I lowered down the camera to the sheet
To show the source of all the rising heat

She stopped the teasing and the little smirk
And watched the way the heavy muscles work
She said the problem was extremely real
And wanted to observe the way I feel She told me
I should move from left to right
To satisfy her hunger and her sight

She took her shirt and pulled it off her head
To show the heavy gravity in bed
She licked her thumb and touched her nipple hard
She did not keep a single inch of guard
She slid her hand between her open thighs
I watched the hunger in her lovely eyes

She told me I should touch myself right now
I wiped the sweat from off my heavy brow
She asked me what I wanted to do there
I told her I would strip her body bare
I'd put her on the counter by the sink
And give her not a moment left to think

I said I'd lick the melting sweet ice cream

And make her shout and very loudly scream
I promised I would slap her with the meat
Until the redness made the look complete
I'd bury it inside her very deep
A memory that she would always keep

She told me I should ruin her today
She did not want to stop or to delay
She opened up her mouth upon the screen
The most exciting sight I've ever seen
I let the heavy fluid start to fly
And let out such a heavy happy cry

We lay there breathing in the morning sun
The heavy work of pleasure was all done
She wiped the sweat and gave a little smile
We rested for a very little while
She said next time she wants to feel the skin
And let the real life pleasure now begin

5. SHE SUCKED MY DICK IN IBIZA

In search of fun and endless delights,
I traveled to Ibiza for summer nights,
Little did I know, I'd meet a goddess in red,
A throat queen that left me breathless in bed.

On my last night out with my travel mate,
We sought out drinks to celebrate,
Two ladies approached with a curious gaze,
Assessing us from head to toe in many ways.

NATE HALIV: PLEASE EXCUSE ME FOR NOT BEING SHAKESPEARE

With no doubt, they knew we were blessed,
The blonde joined my friend, and I was impressed,
With the red-haired girl who sat beside me,
Her curves barely hidden, a seductive spree.

We flirted and bantered for a few,
And then she made an offer I couldn't refuse,
For €100, she promised a trip to heaven,
And I eagerly accepted without hesitation.

She followed me to my room with grace,
A daughter of Delilah, a captivating face,
She grabbed my crotch with a gentle squeeze,
Causing me to moan and gasp with ease.

"Welcome to Ibiza," she whispered with glee,
As she unbuckled my belt with a key,
Releasing my pink monster from its cage,
Her eyes widening with surprise and amaze.

"I see the good Lord has endowed you greatly,"
She said with a smile, which left me dazed and hazy,
Then she pushed me gently onto the bed,
And began stroking my dick with both hands instead.

She licked my balls with a devilish tongue,
Sending sensations to my core that left me undone,
My soul sucked out of me with each deep breath,
As I poured my essence over her like a hot caress.

She washed her face and dressed up to leave,
But as a gentleman, I knew what to achieve,

NATE HALIV: PLEASE EXCUSE ME FOR NOT BEING SHAKESPEARE

I couldn't let her go without a proper goodbye,
So, I made her relax and lay back with a sigh.
Starting from her breasts and down to her thighs,
I kissed her with passion that brought tears to her eyes,
Her labia folds I parted with gentle fingers,
Before diving in with my tongue that still lingers.

She squirted twice, like a fountain of wet dreams,
Her moans of ecstasy music to my ears, it seems,
Pinching her nipples softly, I kept eating with glee,
Her love professed for me like an endless sea.

When I was done pleasing her with my tongue,
I felt the urge to take her with my mighty lung,
I reached for a condom, but she wanted it raw,
On the pill and disease-free, she said with a draw.

I rammed my dick into her with all my strength,
Three deep strokes and two shallow, in great length,
Massaging her breasts, I sent her to heaven with glee,
She squirted three times on my pink monster that set her free.

When we were done, she asked if I had a woman,
But I ignored her and slept, feeling like a true champion,
Replenishing my strength, for Ibiza is a wild ride,
And with her, I had an experience that I couldn't hide.

6. THE VEILED VIRGIN

Freshman year.
There was a girl in my Civics class named Zahra.
She was a ghost in the back row,
Always draped in black fabric from head to toe,
Only her eyes visible, dark and watchful.

The other guys made jokes,
Called her a ninja, laughed when she walked by.
I didn't laugh.
I just held the door.

It started with a mistake.
A stupid, early morning slip of the thumb.
I meant to send a picture of my morning wood to a girl I was seeing,
A classic "good morning" Snapchat text.
Instead, it went to my Campus Story.

I deleted it in ten seconds,
My heart hammering against my ribs,
But the damage was done.
Three views. And one of them was Zahra.

I expected her to report me.
Or at least avoid me.
But the next day, she walked right up to my desk.
She didn't look down.
She looked right at me, a tiny smile crinkling the corners of her eyes.
"The weather is nice today, isn't it?" she asked.
We had never spoken about the weather.
We both knew what she was really talking about.
"Come over tonight," she whispered,

NATE HALIV: PLEASE EXCUSE ME FOR NOT BEING SHAKESPEARE

Sliding a piece of paper onto my notebook.
"We can study."

Her apartment was small,
Smelling of cardamom and old books.
I sat on the edge of a beige loveseat.
She sat next to me. Too close.
Her thigh pressed against mine,
The fabric of her abaya rough against my jeans.
"I saw it," she said, handing me a cup of coffee.
She didn't blush. She was deadly serious.
"I saw what you posted.
And I haven't stopped thinking about it."

She set the coffee down and turned to face me.
"I want you, Nate. I want that thing inside me."
She took a breath, her voice trembling just a little.
"But I can't. Not the way you want."
She explained it like a business transaction.
The religion. The family expectation.
The blood on the sheets on the wedding night.

She had to be a virgin for her husband.
"But," she said, grabbing my hand and placing it over her heart,
"The rules don't say anything about the back door."
I stared at her.
The quiet, religious girl from the back row was asking me to ruin her.

She stood up and reached for the pins.
The veil fell first. Then the robe.
It was like unboxing a secret.
Underneath all that black cloth, she was magnificent.

NATE HALIV: PLEASE EXCUSE ME FOR NOT BEING SHAKESPEARE

Skin like honey, curves that the fabric had completely hidden.
Her breasts were heavy, spilling out of a lace bra
I never would have guessed she owned.

She didn't wait for me to undress her.
She got on her hands and knees on the rug,
Looking back at me over her shoulder.
"Show me," she demanded.
"Tear me open."

I didn't need to be told twice.
I slicked up,
The room suddenly feeling very small and very hot.
I lined it up and pushed.
She gasped, a sharp, high-pitched yelp of pain
But she pushed back against me.
It was tight. Very tight.
I had to go slow, letting her adjust,
Listening to her breathing shift from pain to heavy, rhythmic panting.

I used my hands, my mouth,
Easing the tension until she was begging for the friction.
"Harder," she moaned, her forehead pressed against the carpet.
"Don't treat me like I'm fragile."
I let go. I drove into her with everything I had,
The visual of her—unveiled and raveled—driving me over the edge.
It was raw. It was perfect. Until she ruined it.

She turned her head,
Sweat sticking her hair to her face, eyes rolled back in ecstasy.
"Yes, Nate! Yes!" she screamed.
"I love you! I love this! I love you!"

NATE HALIV: PLEASE EXCUSE ME FOR NOT BEING SHAKESPEARE

The words hit me like a bucket of ice water.
Love. My erection died instantly.
It went from a moment of pure physical heat
To a suffocating trap in one second.

I hate that word.
I hate the clinginess, the expectation,
The delusion of it.
I pulled out, leaving her empty and panting on the floor.

"Nate?" she asked, her voice hazy.
I didn't answer.
I zipped up my jeans, grabbed my bag, and walked to the door.
"Where are you going?" she called out,
Confusion creeping into her tone.
I didn't look back.
I just closed the door,
Leaving her to wonder why the fantasy ended the moment.

7. A BUS TRIP TO LAGOS

The bus was cramped and smelled like diesel and sweat,
Bound for Lagos under a sun that didn't care.
I was jammed into the back row,
Shoulder-to-shoulder with a girl who looked like a dream.

She was wearing a skirt that ended way too high
And a blouse so thin it was basically just a suggestion.
I could see the dark circles of her nipples through the fabric,
Heavy and swaying with every pothole we hit.

NATE HALIV: PLEASE EXCUSE ME FOR NOT BEING SHAKESPEARE

The road was rough, and our skin kept brushing.
Every time the driver slammed the brakes,
Her thigh would press against mine. Burning hot.
I looked over and saw her phone.
She wasn't hiding it. She was watching a video,
Something explicit and loud,
Her eyes glazed over as she stared at the screen.

She reached up, slid a hand under her blouse,
And started twisting her nipple right there in the open.
I leaned in, the noise of the engine drowning out my voice.
"You look like you could use some help with that," I whispered.

She didn't even hesitate.
She looked me dead in the eyes, her breath hitching.
"Yes," she said. "Please."
She shifted, spreading her legs just enough.

I pulled my backpack onto my lap
To hide us from the rest of the bus,
Tucking it over her knees like a tent.
I reached under the bag, my hand finding her breast.
It was warm and soft, the nipple already a hard peak in my palm.
She let out a low moan,
Her head falling back onto my shoulder
As the bus rattled down the highway.

She leaned in and bit my earlobe, hard.
"Go lower," she hissed.
My hand slid down her stomach,
Under the lace of her panties.
She was already slick. Completely soaked.

NATE HALIV: PLEASE EXCUSE ME FOR NOT BEING SHAKESPEARE

I found the center of her and started to work,
My fingers moving in a steady, rhythmic circle.
She was loud now, her moans getting dangerously high.
The old woman in the seat in front of us turned around,
But all she saw was my bag and two people "sleeping."

I pulled my finger out, glistening and wet,
And held it to her lips.
"Taste yourself," I told her.
She closed her eyes and sucked my finger clean,
Her tongue swirling around the tip while she stared at me.

"My turn," she whispered.
She reached over and undid my belt,
Her hands quick and practiced.
Under the cover of the bag, she leaned down,
Her braids brushing my lap as she took me in.

The sensation was incredible.
The heat of her mouth
Mixed with the vibration of the bus on the asphalt.
She used her hand to cup me,
Her thumb tracing the base,
Bringing me right to the edge as we crossed the city limits.

I finished under that bag,
My eyes closed tight,
Listening to the rhythmic thump-thump of the tires on the road.
She sat back up, wiped her mouth with the back of her hand,
And gave me a small, satisfied smirk.

When the bus finally pulled into the terminal,

The doors hissed open and the chaos of Lagos poured in.
We stood up, straightened our clothes, and adjusted our bags.
"Have a good life, Nate," she said,
Though I never told her my name.

She disappeared into the crowd before I could even respond.
I don't know who she was,
And I'll never see her again,
But I'll never forget that ride.

8. THE NASTY TRUST FUND GIRL

We matched on Bumble right away
She had no time for games or play
She wanted someone bold and rough
A guy who liked the nasty stuff
I told her I was just the guy
And that I would not be too shy

We met to eat a fancy meal
She looked consistent with the deal
Her skin was pale and very chic
Her expensive style was quite unique
With jewelry worth a massive price
And shoes that looked so very nice

She told me what she planned to do
While we enjoyed the barbecue
Her dad had cheated on his wife
She wanted to disrupt his life
She did not need a friend or guide
She needed anger on her side

NATE HALIV: PLEASE EXCUSE ME FOR NOT BEING SHAKESPEARE

I reached beneath the table then
To touch her skin right there and then
I found no underwear or lace
Just bare skin in that public place
She gasped but did not push me back
She liked the sudden bold attack

We went to use the bathroom stall
And stood against the marble wall
She asked if I was clean and fit
I nodded as she handled it
She called her dad upon the phone
And placed it on the floor alone

Her dad said "Hello" on the call
He did not understand at all
I moved in close and did my part
To help her break her father's heart
She screamed my name for him to hear
And made the message very clear

Her father yelled confused and scared
But neither one of us had cared
She shook and dropped down to the floor
She could not take it anymore
She said that I was very great
And happy that we had this date

She fixed her hair and fixed her skirt
No longer looking hurt or curt
She said that we were fully done
And that she'd had her bit of fun

She paid the bill and walked away
To end our very crazy day

9. THE RECEPTIONIST

I went to France one sunny day
In a hotel where rich folks stay
The lobby floor was white and clean
The girl inside was tall and lean
She told me what the room would cost
I paid the price and did not pause

I asked to have her phone right then
She looked around and grabbed a pen
She said the rules were very strict
But liked the man that she had picked
She wrote the digits on a sheet
And said exactly when to meet

I called her later that same night
To make sure everything was right
I told her I just want some fun
Before the morning rise of sun
We picked a different place to go
So people there would never know

She showed up in a dress of black
With nothing holding on the back
She looked so good I had to stare
At all the beauty standing there
I pulled her in across the floor

NATE HALIV: PLEASE EXCUSE ME FOR NOT BEING SHAKESPEARE

And quickly locked the heavy door

She fell down quickly to her knees
And aimed to satisfy and please
She knew exactly what to do
The moment was amazing too
I held her head and felt the rush
Inside the room meant for a hush

I turned her over on the sheet
The moment really was so sweet
She made a quiet gasping sound
As we were moving all around
It felt much better than a scream
Like waking from a lovely dream

She took control and climbed above
We made a fierce and wild love
She knew the way to move just right
We stayed awake throughout the night
We did it four more times or so
Until the sun began to glow

We dressed when morning light came in
To end our night of fun and sin
She fixed her hair and walked away
To start her very normal day
I saw her working at the stand
Just like the night that we had planned

10. I LIKE TO WATCH

I am not strange or sick inside my mind
At least not in the way that most will find
I love to see you with another guy
To watch him use you while I stand nearby
It does not make me mad to see the sight
It makes me ready for the coming night

I came home early on a Thursday past
I did not want the quiet peace to last
I did not speak or make a single sound
Until a rhythmic thumping noise
I found I walked into the hallway in the gloom
And stopped outside the open guest bed room

I opened up the door a little bit
To see the way the two of you would fit
I saw his face between your open thighs
And heard the pleasure in your happy cries
He was a man of heavy distinct size
I watched him claim the beauty of his prize

My hand went down inside my denim pants
As I observed the rhythm of your dance
The jealousy did not appear at all
I stood alone against the darkened wall
I do not care regarding who he is
I only want to see you become his

Your heart is mine to keep and always hold
But sharing bodies never will get old
I love to watch a stranger make you wet

A visual I never will forget
I love to see a woman taste your skin
And watch the lovely trouble you are in

So do not hide the text or sneaky call
You do not need to hide the truth at all
Just leave the bedroom door unlocked for me
And open up the blinds so I can see
Invite them in to have their way with you
And let me watch the dirty things you do

11. NOT THE TYPE

I am the one you should not love at all
Let's get this straight before we start to fall
I will not send a text to say hello
Or ask about the places that you go
I send a photo in the morning light
To show you my desire is at its height

I will not bring you flowers for the vase
Instead I bring a bag of silk and lace
It is a gift that costs a heavy price
But ripping it apart will feel so nice
My teeth will tear the fabric off your skin
Before the heavy action can begin

We go to movies sitting in the back
But watching screens is something that we lack
My hand will slide up high upon your thigh
Until you let a heavy breath and sigh
I do not want to hold your tiny hand

I want to make you ache at my command

Do not use words like love or care for me
That is a trap from which I always flee
I will not heal the scars regarding men
Or hear about your exes once again
But when the lust is keeping you awake
Just call me for the pleasure that we make

I do not care regarding hair or nails
Or listening to all your daily tales
Just send a picture of the sexy clothes
And strike a very naughty naked pose
Just spread your legs and open up so wide
I want to see the way you look inside

I am not here to hold your beating heart
We knew that this was true right from the start
I am not here to heal your ugly scars
Or talk about the planet and the stars
But when you need rough sex to ease the pain
You know just how to find me once again

12. A GIRL AFTER MY HEART
You are the only one who understands
Exactly what the situation demands
You do not ask for texts or look for signs
You do not read between the spoken lines
You know your place is here inside the dark
Without a question or a single spark

NATE HALIV: PLEASE EXCUSE ME FOR NOT BEING SHAKESPEARE

I called you late at night with nothing said
I did not ask if you were in your bed
You whispered that the door was open wide
So I could walk right into you inside
You crawled across the rug on hands and knees
And used your mouth to satisfy and please

My voice alone can make your engine start
We do not need a loving mind or heart
The sheets were wet before I touched your skin
Before the real action could begin
You did not say you're sorry for the mess
You only wanted more and nothing less

Come over to my house again tonight
You know the rules and how to do it right
Leave all your phones inside the parked sedan
And do not deviate from my set plan
Knock on the door six times and walk inside
Take off your clothes with nothing left to hide

I sit inside the chair to watch you work
It is a duty that you never shirk
Use fingers till I hear the sloppy sound
And move your body all along the ground
Pull up your knees so I can see the view
I want to finish deep inside of you

And here is where the other women fail
They want a happy ending or a tale
We will not cuddle when the act is done
The timer starts before the rise of sun

You grab your keys and walk out of the door
Until I call you back to give me more

13. MAKEUP SEX

Please stay a little mad and do not smile
I want to keep the tension for a while
I love the way your jaw is looking tight
It feels just like a storm before the night
We settle things when yelling goes away
And clothes come off to end the angry day

You stood beside the bed to list my crimes
And told me I was wrong a dozen times
I walked to you and did not say a word
Your angry voice was not a thing I heard
I touched the spot that makes you feel so weak
And stopped the angry words you tried to speak

The anger faded from your lovely eyes
I went to get a cold and sweet surprise
I brought vanilla cream out from the cold
To do exactly what I had been told
I poured the scoop upon your center part
To finish what we were about to start

I knelt between your thighs upon the floor
Just like a holy altar I adore
I hid an ice cube underneath my tongue
To keep the feeling sharp and very young
I licked the cream and found the magic spot
While grabbing at the chest that you have got

NATE HALIV: PLEASE EXCUSE ME FOR NOT BEING SHAKESPEARE

You let a sudden rush come out so fast
I caught it all and made the moment last
I kissed your lips so you could taste the treat
To make the dirty moment full and sweet
I asked you if the anger was still there
You shook your head and grabbed my messy hair

I picked you up and pinned you to the wall
We did not have a chance to slip or fall
You wrapped your legs around my waist so tight
To finish off the angry fight tonight
The thumping sound was music to my ear
As I removed the last of every tear

We finished up and rested head to head
You said that you forgave the things I said
I pulled away to finish on your skin
To end the night of anger and of sin
We do not need to talk about the fight
This is the way to make the wrong things right

14. DRUGS AND SEX

I took the kit to give myself a start
And wake the beating of my heavy heart
The needle felt so cold inside my hand
Exactly as the evening had been planned
The hit of meth was sharp and very clear
To take away the fog and every fear

I slowly took the fabric off her skin
To let the naked moment now begin

NATE HALIV: PLEASE EXCUSE ME FOR NOT BEING SHAKESPEARE

She calmed me like some marijuana smoke
And all the heavy sleeping hunger woke
The sight was better than the MDMA
To light the fire in a different way

I told her to get down upon the floor
She knew exactly what I waited for
She focused like she took an Adderall
And did not let the concentration fall
I held her hair to keep her in the place
And saw the focus on her pretty face
I pushed her back upon the pillowcase
And put my face inside her secret place
I breathed her in to feel the heavy burn
And waited for the tide to finally turn
It felt just like a line of white cocaine
To rush inside the heavy blood and vein

I told her she should climb on top of me
To ride and set the heavy spirit free
She moved with danger like a lethal dose
We kept the bodies very tight and close
It felt just like the drug of fentanyl
With power that could make a giant fall

I stayed inside to feel the heroin peace
And let the heavy frantic movements cease
I saw the colors of an LSD
That floated in the air for me to see
I fell into a heavy codeine sleep
Into a slumber that was dark and deep

NATE HALIV: PLEASE EXCUSE ME FOR NOT BEING SHAKESPEARE

15. STAY MAD

Vanessa is not like the other girls
She does not care for jewelry or pearls
The other girl forgives me way too fast
But anger here is really built to last
I stand outside her door at two a.m.
I do not want the easy likes of them
She cracked the door but kept the metal chain
She looked at me with anger and disdain
She told me to go home and let her be
I said that she was just the girl for me
I touched her jaw and said I like the fight
I want to be with you this very night

She slammed the door and took the chain away
She told me she had nothing left to say
She walked into the kitchen down the hall
And stood against the granite kitchen wall
She crossed her arms and looked at me with hate
She did not want a lover or a mate

I walked to her and lifted up her gown
She did not smile but kept an angry frown
She was not wet or ready for the deed
She did not feel the passion or the need
She whispered that she hated me so much
I said that she should focus on my touch

I put her on the counter with a crash
The bowls of fruit fell down with quite a smash
I entered her and did not take it slow
I wanted her to feel the heavy blow

She bit my shoulder hard and made it bleed
She scratched my back to satisfy her need

She told me to say sorry to her face
I said that was not happening in this place
I drove it deep inside to make her scream
Just like a violent and crazy dream
She finished with a jagged shout of pain
Like she was going totally insane

She pushed me back when we were fully done
She did not say that she had any fun
She told me to get out and leave the place
With anger still appearing on her face
She said she still has not forgiven me
And told me I should go and let her be

I zipped my jeans and felt the scratching sting
I did not care about a single thing
I smiled at her standing in the mess
She looked so good inside her silky dress
I said that I would see her the next day
To have another fight in the same way

16. BELLA

She does not want the soft and gentle talk
She does not want a slow and steady walk
She paces in the room upon the floor
And waits for me to walk inside the door
She wears her heels and gives a hungry stare
She hunts me like a lion in the lair

NATE HALIV: PLEASE EXCUSE ME FOR NOT BEING SHAKESPEARE

She told me not to stand there on the rug
She did not want a kiss or gentle hug
She turned her back and held the wooden shelf
She looked as if she surely pleased herself
She said she waited for an hour long
And knew exactly what was going wrong

I dropped my keys upon the table top
I knew that she would never let me stop
I lifted up her skirt to find my way
She was so wet and ready for the play
I entered her and made the bookshelf shake
It felt like something that was bound to break

She told me she would like it very hard
I grabbed her hips and played my simple card
I pulled her back against my chest and skin
To push the heavy feeling deeper in
The rhythm was so messy and so fast
I wondered how the wooden shelf would last

She pulled away and pushed me to the seat
To find a better way to feel the heat
She climbed on top and straddled on my waist
We did not have a moment we could waste
She started riding with a steady pace
I saw the look of need upon her face

She told me to look deep inside her eyes
They held the heat that burns and never dies
She touched herself to find the rhythm right
She squeezed me with her body very tight

She let a scream go echoing around
It was a jagged and a lovely sound

I held her waist and anchored her right down
I finished deep inside without a frown
She fell against my chest and rested there
With sweat upon her skin and in her hair
She bit my lip and reached to get her dress
And said next week we make another mess

17. I DON'T CUDDLE

The room was quiet save the cooling air
The sheets were tangled in a messy snare
I felt her body moving close to mine
To cross the very strictly drawn line
She tried to rest her head beneath my chin
And trap me in the state that we were in

I sat up straight and reached to grab my clock
She looked as if she truly felt the shock
She asked me if I would not stay a while
I did not offer her a happy smile
I told her that the rules are very clear
I do not stay to hold you close and dear

She said I screamed her name a moment past
And thought the loving feeling meant to last
I laughed and told her it was just a sound
Because the perfect friction had been found
It is a simple thing biology
And not a sign of love for you to see

NATE HALIV: PLEASE EXCUSE ME FOR NOT BEING SHAKESPEARE

I stood to put my denim pants back on
The feeling of the moment was all gone
We made a deal the night we first had met
A promise that you never should forget
But women always try to find a crack
To keep me there and hold my body back

I love the way you move and what you do
It feels amazing being inside you
But loving is a word I do not say
It implies that I am inclined to stay
The physical is all I want to see
The rest is not a thing that works for me

She watched me as I tied my heavy shoe
She asked if I was truly almost through
I kissed her on the head and said goodbye
I did not want to hear her start to cry
I said I call when I have got the urge
Before the feelings start to rise and surge

I walked outside into the cool night air
I did not have a single worry there
It felt much better than the heated bed
I cleared the thoughts inside my heavy head
I do not settle and I do not stay
I do the deed and then I fly away

18. THROAT GODDESS

She is nineteen, quite young and small but very tough
She knows exactly how to do her stuff
She walks inside and drops her heavy bag
And does not let the passing moment lag
She ties her hair back in a sturdy knot
To show me all the skills that she has got

I sat upon the leather chair that night
And watched her move into the fading light
She is so small but she is in command
She started softly with her tiny hand
She looked up at me with a focused stare
While kneeling down upon the carpet there

She leaned right in and opened up so wide
To take the heavy length deep down inside
She did not pause or hesitate a bit
She made sure that the two of us would fit
I gripped the leather armrest with my hand
Because the feeling was so very grand

She asked me if I liked it with a hum
She made the feeling vibrate and go numb
I could not speak or hardly even breathe
I felt the pressure swell and start to seethe
She wiggled back and forth upon the floor
And used the friction till I wanted more

She used her hands to guide me deeper still
Her eyes on mine to test my strength of will
I could not last for very long that way

NATE HALIV: PLEASE EXCUSE ME FOR NOT BEING SHAKESPEARE

I let the pleasure have the final say
I arched my back and let the fluid go
She took it all and did not stop the flow

She pulled away and sat back on the floor
She looked as if she wanted even more
The messy fluid dripped upon her chin
She gave a smile regarding all my sin
She wiped it off and went to get a drink
Before I had a moment just to think

I stayed inside the chair to rest my legs
And drank the pleasure to the very dregs
Most women make a man feel very fine
But she is truly top of all the line
The throat goddess is who she is to me
Next week I will return for her to see

19. MINE FOR THE NIGHT

Tonight, you're mine, my sweet delight
I've paid the price, now it's time to begin our sexual flight

Submit to me, obey my will
For I am your master, yours to thrill

Strip off your clothes
Let me see you naked

Lie on the bed, spread those legs wide
Play with the bean between your legs,
Don't stop until I decide

NATE HALIV: PLEASE EXCUSE ME FOR NOT BEING SHAKESPEARE

Come to me. Wrap your tongue around my dick.
Swallow my seeds, let them fill your mouth

Let me bury myself inside you
Yes, that's it, your tightness burns like fire
Stand up, grab the table
Wait, let me put some lubricant first

Good girl. Turn around. Let me enter from behind
Yes, that's it. You're one of a kind

Hang your leg on my shoulder
Hold me tight, let me enter you

Bite me, scratch me
Tell me to go harder, faster, deeper

The heaven between your legs is so sweet,
I don't mind getting lost
Touch your toes.
Now wiggle a little to the left
Yes, just like that
Keep bouncing on it
Yes, I like the friction

Take it all, make me whole
Let me pour it on your face
Evidence of my hard work
Let me see those whitish stains on your face and stomach

You're a good girl,
Daddy's little slut

20. MY TEXAS COWGIRL

I met her at a bar near Austin town
She was a girl who never would back down
She looked like she had worked out in the sun
And not like girls who only want some fun
We went inside her ranch so far away
She pushed me down and told me I must stay

She told me I was in her house right now
She did not want a gentle lover vow
She grabbed a leather whip beside the door
To tease me as I lay upon the floor
It stung my chest and made my heart beat fast
I knew the gentle time was in the past

She told me I must call her Ma'am out loud
She stood before me tall and very proud
She took off clothes to show her muscle lines
She did not look for sweet romantic signs
She pinned my arms and climbed upon my waist
We did not have a moment we could waste

She rode me like a horse she had to break
She did not care how much my shoulders ache
She dug her nails into my skin so deep
A memory that I would always keep
She told me not to move until she said
And spun the shadows round above my head

The friction was so raw and very rough
She could not seem to ever get enough
She did not want a romance or a date

She only wanted to control her fate
I watched the sweat collect upon her skin
As she enjoyed the trouble we were in

She arched her back and let a heavy cry
It echoed in the house and to the sky
I finished then and grabbed her by the side
Enjoying every moment of the ride
I smelled the scent of cedar and of sweat
A moment that I never will forget

She stood and wiped the sweat away from her
And acted like the sex was just a blur
She said that I had been a decent ride
But now I had to go and step outside
She had some work to do at rise of sun
And told me that our time was fully done

I walked to find my car in Texas night
And felt the stinging of the whip and bite
I do not know if this is love or lust
But coming back is something that I must
I know that I will go back to her side
The next time that she wants to take a ride

21. TWO WOMEN, ONE MAN

The hotel room in Dallas was so dim
The lights were shining on the window rim
One girl was tall with skin of deep dark brown
The other was the smallest girl in town

NATE HALIV: PLEASE EXCUSE ME FOR NOT BEING SHAKESPEARE

They watched to see if I could handle it
I walked toward the bed to simply sit

I called for Keisha first to come to me
She moved with fluid grace for me to see
She sat upon my lap and felt the heat
The moment was already very sweet
I looked at Becky standing by the wall
And told her she should answer to my call

I pulled the second woman to the bed
And placed a pillow underneath her head
I used my hand to make her feel the fire
And satisfy her body and desire
Then Keisha moved her hips to take me in
To start the night of pleasure and of sin

I managed both of them with careful skill
To give them both a very happy thrill
I kissed the neck of Keisha on the right
While Becky held the sheets with all her might
The room was filled with gasps and happy sounds
As we began the very heavy rounds

I moved to Becky and I raised her legs
She looked like someone who just pleads and begs
I entered her with strokes so deep and long
The feeling was so heavy and so strong
I told the other girl to watch the show
And see the rhythm moving fast and slow

When Becky finished shaking on the sheet

NATE HALIV: PLEASE EXCUSE ME FOR NOT BEING SHAKESPEARE

I did not stop or miss a single beat
I turned to Keisha and I spun her round
Until a better angle could be found
I gripped her hips and satisfied her lust
With every single deep and heavy thrust

The air was humid at the hour of three
The girls were lying there in front of me
I used my tongue to clean them very well
And put them both beneath a magic spell
They writhed around and begged for me to stop
Until the heavy energy could drop

I walked to see the empty city street
The cooling air was very nice and sweet
The bed behind was tangled in a mess
I felt the satisfaction and success
I climbed back in to sleep and close my eyes
Beneath the dark and starry Texas skies

22. ALL I WANT FOR CHRISTMAS

I do not care for lights upon the tree
Or opening the gifts for me to see
I want the three Latinas here tonight
To make the winter evening hot and bright
I want the fire of their golden skin
And let the Christmas season now begin

I stood inside the room and shed my shirt
These women love to play and love to flirt
Lucia dropped her dress of silky red

NATE HALIV: PLEASE EXCUSE ME FOR NOT BEING SHAKESPEARE

And knelt before me just like I had said
She used her mouth to start the heavy play
In her specific spicy Latin way

I sat upon the chair to take a seat
She did not miss a single rhythmic beat
Elena climbed on top to ride my lap
While Sofia fell into the honey trap
My fingers slid inside her wetness deep
To wake the hunger from a winter sleep

I whispered Merry Christmas to the ear
The best event of all the current year
She bit my shoulder hard to leave a mark
Inside the middle of the heavy dark
The bodies pressed on every side
There was no place for anyone to hide

We moved the party to the heavy bed
To do exactly what the voices said
I took Lucia from the rear attack
And watched the arching of her lovely back
The headboard banged against the sturdy wall
She gave a very loud and happy call

I gave the pleasure to the other two
Exactly as I promised I would do
I made sure that they all were satisfied
With nothing left for them to keep inside
The room was smelling like the sweat and musk
From early evening to the morning dusk

I finished with the women in a pile
And rested for a very little while
They fell asleep with breathing soft and deep
Into a heavy satisfaction sleep
I do not need a present with a bow
These three Latinas are the gift I know

23. YOUR CREAM

All I desire is when our bodies meet
To feel the rising of the heavy heat
I do not care for poetry or rhyme
I only want to have a heavy time
Your love spot is a destination true
A wet and rhythmic place inside of you

I think regarding how we were before
And how we moved across the wooden floor
I watched your eyes roll back inside your head
With every movement in the heavy bed
The white and magic fluid starts to flow
To let the heavy satisfaction show

I sat you on the dresser on the side
And opened up your heavy legs so wide
I used my fingers with a steady flick
To make the juices flow so white and thick
I leaned right down to have a little taste
We did not have a moment we could waste

I entered you again to feel the glide
With nothing left for you to try and hide

NATE HALIV: PLEASE EXCUSE ME FOR NOT BEING SHAKESPEARE

The cream allowed me to go very deep
A memory that I will always keep
Your thighs were clamping tight around my waist
While I enjoyed the fluid and the taste

I drove into you till the room was loud
The heavy feeling was a thunder cloud
I wanted you to let the river go
And let the heavy juices start to flow
The sheets were ruined by the wet and stain
There was no pleasure that we could restrain

This is the only thing I truly need
To satisfy the heavy hunger greed
I come back for the flavor and the sight
Of you exploding in the heavy night
So roll your eyes and let the feeling take
The only magic that we ever make

24. TIANA THE STALLION

I thought that I was scary in the bed
I thought that I was strong in heart and head
Then Tiana came with skin of golden brown
The smallest little lady in the town
I thought that I would break her tiny frame
And that she could not play the heavy game

I asked her if she truly could withstand
The heavy pressure of my heavy hand
She sat upon the mattress on the floor
And kicked her shoes right over by the door

NATE HALIV: PLEASE EXCUSE ME FOR NOT BEING SHAKESPEARE

She told me I should find out for myself
And put my foolish doubts upon the shelf

I gave her everything I had inside
I took her on a forty minute ride
I used my weight and every ounce of strength
I went to every single depth and length
I gasped for air and sweat ran down my face
I thought that I had surely won the race

But she was lying there and smiling sweet
She did not look exhausted by the heat
She looked as if she took a little walk
While I could barely find the breath to talk
She asked me if that really was the end
And if I had no energy to spend

She flipped me over on my heavy back
And started on her own intense attack
She was a stallion riding in the night
She held me in her grip so very tight
She rode me with a power strong and fast
I knew my energy could never last

She told me stories lying in the dark
That really made a frightening sort of mark
She said she handled seven men or eight
And never even emptied out her plate
She said it was a casual event
Until the men were absolutely spent

I looked at her and felt a little fear

To see the beast that was beside me here
She is an athlete of the highest grade
The finest lover that was ever made
I am no monster in the room tonight
It is Tiana who brings all the fright

25. CAN'T LOVE YOU PROPERLY

I'm sorry, babe, I can't love you right,
when this white powder is on my mind.
It gives me relief, God help me,
no woman has ever matched that feeling.

The rush it brings, the sudden lift,
nothing compares to that small hit.
It's where I run, where I disappear,
this coke is always waiting here.

But you, my love, keep raising hell,
while this powder never asks me to explain.
It never shames me or talks back,
it feels more solid than anything I have.

It's my confidant, my quiet place,
my closest friend when the night gets late.
It never gets upset when I go cold,
it never makes me feel less than whole.

When I take it, my head goes quiet,
it pushes back the weight I carry.
This white powder feels like relief,
like something close to belief.

It gives me calm, it gives me edge,
it keeps me standing when I'm close to ledge.
You wish I'd choose you over cocaine,
but this is the only thing that hits my veins.

26. FRIENDS WITH BENEFITS

I liked the way that things between us were
You were a place where I could hide and blur
But then you said you loved me loud and clear
The words I really did not want to hear
It landed like the water very cold
And made the story feel too tired and old

We had a deal we never spoke aloud
To keep our heads within the private cloud
We understood exactly what we had
To bring the feelings makes it very bad
We shared the body and the heavy time
But crossing lines is like a heavy crime

So let us keep it simple and so plain
I do not want to hear you can explain
Just stop the talking and come lie with me
And be the lover that you used to be
Keep out the heart and leave it far away
We only have the body for the play

I do not want the names or softness now
I do not want a single lover's vow
I want the heat and closeness of the night
To make the heavy feeling very right

If you cannot stay inside the line
Then you can be no longer truly mine

So lie back down and let the words all fall
I do not want to hear them not at all
What we are doing has no love in it
So let the pieces of the puzzle fit
It never did and never will be true
That is the way I want to be with you

27. WILD PARTY

The penthouse room was full of neon light
The bass was heavy in the humid night
The smell of perfume hung inside the air
With smoke and bourbon scenting everywhere
I stood inside the center of the beat
And felt the rising of the heavy heat

I grabbed a girl who wore a silver dress
To pull her into all the wild mess
We did not dance but crashed upon the floor
We did not want the talking anymore
The clothes were dropped like artifacts of past
We knew the moment was not built to last

I pulled her to the table made of glass
To watch the heavy moments slowly pass
We bent right down to take the powder white
To make the feeling sharp and very bright
My heart began to vibrate in my chest
We did not want to take a single rest

We caught another body moving by
With hunger showing in her dark brown eye
We did not need to ask the reason why
Or look into the stormy city sky
We pushed the safety measures to the side
And took the risk upon the heavy ride

The music throbbed and pushed us to the peak
We did not have the power left to speak
We tangled up upon the velvet seat
And moved our bodies to the heavy beat
One girl was hanging on my shoulder tight
We burned the center of the crazy night

This was not just a party anymore
It was a fire burning on the floor
Tomorrow did not matter in the least
As we enjoyed the nature of the beast
We flew as high as chemicals allow
And lived entirely inside the now

28. RED LIGHT DISTRICT

November cold in Amsterdam is real
But I can tell just how the districts feel
The neon red spills out upon the street
Where all the hungry people come to meet
I saw my Julie standing in the glass
A beauty that no other could surpass

She wore the lace of black upon her skin
I tapped the glass to let the night begin

NATE HALIV: PLEASE EXCUSE ME FOR NOT BEING SHAKESPEARE

Her hair was burning like a fire red
She smiled at the things I left unsaid
I heard the lock and walked inside the room
To leave the heavy winter and the gloom

The room was clean and smelled of sweet perfume
I paid the cash inside the little room
She dropped the robe to show her curvy shape
There was no way that I could now escape
Her body filled the tiny narrow space
A look of knowing was upon her face

She said she knew exactly who I was
She did not stop or even try to pause
She pushed my shoulders back upon the bed
With burning hair surrounding round my head
She climbed on top and set the rhythm fast
I knew the heavy joy was bound to last

I flipped her over face into the sheet
To make the heavy angle quite complete
I saw the skin so flushed beneath the light
Inside the middle of the heavy night
I drove into her curves and corners deep
A memory that I would always keep

The sounds she made were rough and not a song
We knew we did not have the time for long
I knelt between her thighs to have a taste
With no more time for us to try and waste
She gripped the sheets and felt the sweet release
And finally the heavy movements cease

I stepped back out into the freezing chill
But I could feel the heat inside me still
The tourists walked along the cobbled street
I walked away with steady moving feet
I count the days until I can return
To watch the red and neon fire burn

29. LOVE IS A MYTH

Love is a dream, a fleeting tale
A myth that's spun and doomed to fail
But lust is real, a primal fire
A burning need that won't expire
So spread your legs and let me in
Forget love's lies, embrace the sin
Send me your nudes and let me see
The beauty that lies between your thighs

Don't whisper sweet nothings in my ear
Tell me you want me, loud and clear
No need for love, let's just embrace
The raw and primal lust we chase

Let's rip our clothes and be as one
Forget love's myth, embrace the fun
We'll make love like wild beasts tonight
In every hole, I'll make you mine

So forget love, let's just indulge
In primal lust, let's just be rough
We'll make love like animals tonight
And in our passion, we'll ignite

30. I HEARD YOU LIKE IT BLACK AND LONG

I heard you like it black and long,
A taste for the forbidden, oh so right,
When it comes to that, I do no wrong,
I have something black, huge, and long,
Just the way you crave it at night.

With a crown of pink, a treasure to behold,
You'll find no other can to my rod a candle hold,
Just one night with me, and you'll be sold,
On the saying that, once you've gone black,
You'll never go back.

So come, let me part the velvet folds,
With my long, black rod,
And let the stories be told,
Of how you kept returning, on your own accord,
To the lover who left you wanting more.

Let me make you scream,
As I fill you up, and make all your fantasies real,
With my rod, black as night and long as a dream,
You'll find yourself coming back, again and again.

31. THE LIPS BETWEEN YOUR LEGS

I do not care for flowers or for art
I do not want to play the poet's part
My focus tightens on a specific place
I do not look at just your pretty face
I want the velvet heat between your thighs
It is the only treasure that I prize

NATE HALIV: PLEASE EXCUSE ME FOR NOT BEING SHAKESPEARE

I think about the hotel room we shared
And how the two of us were fully bared
I sat you on the desk of heavy wood
I spread your knees as wide as e'er
I could I leaned right down to taste the warmth inside
Where you have got no secret place to hide

The taste was sweet and faintly metal too
I loved to do the dirty things to you
My tongue began to trace along the line
To make you feel so very good and fine
You grabbed my hair and tried to pull me deep
A memory that I will always keep

I leaned back then to see you open wide
And slipped two of my fingers right inside
I felt the liquid coat my heavy hand
Exactly as the two of us had planned
The paradise was dripping on the seat
To make the messy moment quite complete

I stepped right in to fill the space inside
And take you on a heavy happy ride
I heard the raw and jagged little sound
As we began to pound and grind around
Your lips could not form words or speak a name
Because you were so lost inside the game

I drove into you till the room did shake
And gave you all the pleasure you could take
Your body gripped me tight and held me fast
To make the heavy feeling truly last

I made the lips upon your pretty face
Speak with the lips inside the other place

32. COME UNTO ME, ALL YE THAT NEED ORGASMS

I do not care to be your loving man
Or hold your hand according to the plan
I am the one you call to fix the need
When plastic toys cannot fulfill the deed
If you desire release that makes you weak
Then I am just the person you should seek

A woman came to see me late last night
She thought that she could win the heavy fight
I pushed her back against the wooden door
To show her what the evening had in store
I did not start the moment soft and slow
I wanted all her self control to go

I stayed until the fluid hit the floor
And she was begging me to give her more
The evidence ran down her open thighs
I saw the realization in her eyes
She knew that plastic toys are not the same
As playing in this heavy human game

I put her on the counter made of stone
To hear the heavy breathing and the moan
The cold was sharp against her heated skin
As I began to push it deep within
The sound of slapping skin filled up the room
We banished all the quiet and the gloom

NATE HALIV: PLEASE EXCUSE ME FOR NOT BEING SHAKESPEARE

I held her close unto the very edge
Just like a person standing on a ledge
I waited till she begged for her release
And did not give her any rest or peace
She shook so hard she could not hold on tight
And finished in the middle of the night

So bring the hunger to my open door
If you are wanting something real and more
I treat you gently at the very start
Before I take your boundaries apart
You will forget the men you knew before
When you are lying spent upon the floor

33. THE THING BETWEEN MY LEGS

I do not have to boast or even speak
To make a woman feel extremely weak
I see the way her eyes are open wide
With nothing left for her to keep inside
My boxers hit the floor and then they stare
At what is waiting for the women there

They call the thing a monster and are right
It fills the room with heavy power and might
I met a girl who acted cool and tough
And thought that she had surely seen enough
But when she saw the size of what I got
She seemed to freeze right there upon the spot

It pushes past the limits that they keep
And wakes the hunger that is fast asleep

NATE HALIV: PLEASE EXCUSE ME FOR NOT BEING SHAKESPEARE

I watch the saints turn into sinners fast
Because the holy feelings cannot last
Their backs will arch and voices start to break
With all the heavy pleasure that they take

There is no place for logic or for prayer
When we are stripped and naked standing there
The ego and control are stripped away
There is no game that we pretend to play
Lord have some mercy on the ones who try
To walk away and hold their head up high

They try to leave and act like they are fine
But realize that they are truly mine
Their legs are shaking when they walk away
They text me back because they want to stay
It is not only pleasure but command
A force that they can never quite withstand

So keep your woman far away from me
Unless you want to set her spirit free
Because if she comes in this room tonight
And sees the heavy monster in the light
She will not look at you the same again
Or want to be with any other men

34. ONCE UPON A PLAYBOY

I used to be the guy who played the part
I gave a woman all my beating heart
I brought the flowers and the chocolate sweet
I worshipped her and sat beneath her feet
I thought that if I did the good things right
The future would be happy and so bright

But I was wrong about the way of love
It was not sent from angels up above
The first one shattered me and made me cry
I found that she was living out a lie
The baby growing deep inside her womb
Was not my child and sealed my heavy doom

The second woman looked me in the eye
And told me I was just a boring guy
She said she wanted chaos and a storm
And did not like the safety of the norm
She left me for a man who treated bad
And took away the joy I thought we had

The third one was the one to end the show
She struck the final fatal heavy blow
She had a sugar daddy in the town
And slept with all the other men around
I saw the texts and knew that it was true
The gentleman I was is finally through

I realized trust is just a weak mistake
A risk that I am not prepared to take
I do not buy the flowers for the vase

I send a text to meet me at my place
It is much better that I walk away
Than wait for someone who will go astray

A woman told me she was different now
I did not care regarding why or how
She reached to touch my hand and feel the skin
I showed her how the pleasure could begin
I moved her hand onto my leather belt
To stop the feelings that she might have felt

I traded loyal love for power and might
I traded sweet forever for the night
The love has lost the sting it used to give
Because I changed the way I choose to live
I break the hearts of others in the game
And do not feel a single bit of shame

35. YOUNG, WILD, AND HORNY

I found a girl who likes the stash I hold
She does not do exactly as she's told
She looks at it just like a menu list
A chance for fun that never should be missed
We share a hunger for the heavy high
And want to float beneath the open sky

I sat her down upon the messy bed
To calm the thoughts inside her pretty head
I placed a pill of pink inside her hand
She understood exactly what I planned
We rolled a smoke to help us feel the peak

NATE HALIV: PLEASE EXCUSE ME FOR NOT BEING SHAKESPEARE

And take away the words we could not speak

The room began to shake and vibrate fast
We knew the feeling was designed to last
Her eyes were black inside the heavy dark
We felt the rising of the electric spark
I took the vial with a careful touch
To make sure that we did not take too much

We mixed the highs to paint a work of art
To rush the beating of the human heart
A line of white to sharpen up the sight
To make the heavy evening burn so bright
She grabbed my shirt and pulled me to the sheet
To feel the rhythm of the heavy beat

We spent six hours in a lovely daze
Inside the center of the purple haze
The touch was more than it had been before
We rolled around upon the wooden floor
We fused together in a heavy way
Before the coming of the light of day

So take another hit and fly so high
We soar together in the purple sky
Do not be shy my lovely shining light
We own the magic of the crazy night
Let's see how high the two of us can go
Before we have to land and take it slow

36. FOREVER MINE

Even if I share my bed with fifty other women,
You must be exclusive to me
Even if you get horny
And I'm not there with you
You're not allowed to play with yourself
Don't use your toy
You're forbidden to rub your love spot with your fingers

You're mine to touch
Mine to fuck

Other girls can spread their legs wide for me every night
But you're not allowed to spread your legs for another man
You're mine

Call me controlling,
Call me possessive,
I don't mind
You're mine
I will not share

37. DON'T TALK, JUST SUCK

I do not want to hear about your day
I wish for you to put the words away
The conversation is not what I seek
I do not want to hear you start to speak
Just drop down to your knees upon the floor
And be the temptress that I do adore

I know the last time that you tried to fight
You pressed your lips together very tight

NATE HALIV: PLEASE EXCUSE ME FOR NOT BEING SHAKESPEARE

I waited for the anger to be gone
Until the hungry look was fully drawn
You leaned into the silence of the space
A look of hunger was upon your face

I watched you take me deep inside of you
Exactly as I wanted you to do
You looked like you were praying on your knees
In perfect pose to satisfy and please
I leaned back on the sofa made of leather
And held your head to keep us close together

I whispered that you must not say a word
The quiet was the only thing
I heard I felt your tongue begin to trace the line
To send a shiver up the heavy spine
Your fingers moved with care and gentle skill
To give my body such a heavy thrill

You took your time to make the feeling last
The angry words were buried in the past
Your eyes were fixed on mine inside the light
To make the moment feel so very right
There was no tension left inside the place
Just honest hunger on your pretty face

I felt the pressure building to the peak
I did not have the energy to speak
You did not flinch but took the heavy flow
You never let a single droplet go
I am all yours as long as you are still
And use your lips to satisfy my will

38. HER RINGTONE

Her screams echo through the night,
A symphony of pleasure and delight.
Each moan a symphonic note,
As I ravage her body, I gloat.

I nibble on her nipples,
As she gasps in ecstasy,
Her moans turn to soft sobs,
A sign of her vulnerability.
With my fingers, I massage her hidden treasure,
She cries out like a baby, desperate for pleasure.
My tongue on her love spot,
Sends shivers down her body nonstop.

She grips my hair with a fierce fist,
As I thrust deeper, her screams persist.
"Ah Ah Ah," she cries, a crescendo of desire,
As I plow her wet field, like a raging fire.

My neighbors barely sleep a wink,
Due to her ringtone's deafening din,
But I relish in her screams,
For they turn me on like a dream.

39. SHE THOUGHT I WAS LAZY

She thought that I was lazy and quite slow
Until I had a heavy seed to sow
I worked upon her sacred ground with skill
And drove inside to give her quite a thrill
I planted deep inside the warm wet soil

NATE HALIV: PLEASE EXCUSE ME FOR NOT BEING SHAKESPEARE

To show her that I do not fear the toil

She thought that I was lazy not to move
Until I had a point that I could prove
I pinned her back against the heavy wall
And did not let her slip or even fall
I put her leg up high and drove right in
To make her scream regarding all the sin

She thought that I lacked energy and drive
Until I made her count the number five
I used my fingers on her lower lips
And held her steady by her shaking hips
She said that she was thoroughly so pleased
As every bit of tension was released

She thought that I was lazy in the bed
Until I worked to mess inside her head
I used my tongue to bring her to the place
Where only pleasure shows upon her face
She screamed out Daddy in the state of bliss
And gave to me a very sloppy kiss

She thought that I was lazy and too weak
Until I made her lose the will to speak
I took her hard and made her body sore
She could not walk across the wooden floor
For three whole days she wobbled on her feet
Because my lack of lazy was complete

40. THE COST OF LOVE

The cost of love is high, my dear,
It's a price I cannot bear.
For every moment of pleasure,
There's a moment of despair.

The cost of love is heartache,
A pain that cuts like a knife.
It's the fear of losing someone,
It's the struggle for life.
The cost of love is sacrifice,
A giving of oneself.
It's the letting go of ego,
It's the putting of someone else.

The cost of love is trust,
A faith that can be shaken.
It's the risk of being hurt,
It's the fear of being taken.

41. A LOVE LETTER TO FELICIA

I write this note so I do not see you
And all the loving things you try to do
You see a man who is not really there
I cannot handle all the love and care
Your perfect love is something
I must fear I cannot stay another moment here

When I am with you I am someone new
A man who stays to see the morning view
But that old version has been dead for long

To bring him back would be completely wrong
I want the noise and lounges of the night
And keep my freedom in the heavy light

I need to leave before I ruin you
And do the things that I am bound to do
I do not want to say where I have been
Or justify the places and the sin
You talked of futures on the balcony
I only looked for ways that I could flee
I love the chase and strangers in the bed
I cannot get the future in my head
To be with one feels like I choke for air
It is a burden that I cannot bear
I run to find the man I used to be
The one who wants no personality

You are a dove inside a world of pain
I am a monster you cannot restrain
I go to find the next girl and the high
Beneath another city and the sky
Do not await a text or call from me
I am the monster I was born to be

42. MARIJUANA LOVE

I am not good at staying calm and still
I need to feel the heavy rushing thrill
You act just like the weed inside my mind
To leave the heavy static far behind
You are the one temptation I must chase
To find my pleasure in your warm embrace

I hold you close inside my arms tonight
To make sure that I do the rolling right
I pull you in to take away the air
And run my hands across your skin and hair
I want to see you drifting in the zone
Until the world outside is fully gone

I sat against the headboard of the bed
To clear the heavy thoughts inside my head
I asked for you to blow me far away
You did not have a single word to say
Your hair fell down upon my thighs and skin
As you began to take the feeling in

I am addicted to the way it feels
The way your body turns and rocks and reels
I want to put my tongue in every space
And taste the nectar of your secret place
You are the balm that soothes the jagged part
And lights the fire in my heavy heart

I worship how your body moves and shakes
And all the heavy noise your pleasure makes
I hit the spot you try so hard to hide
And keep the rhythm moving deep inside
Let's see how high the two of us can go
Before the morning sun begins to glow

43. THE MYTH OF THE PLAYBOY

He's a creature of legend, a man of myth,
A suave and debonair figure, all too easy to miss.

NATE HALIV: PLEASE EXCUSE ME FOR NOT BEING SHAKESPEARE

He's the life of the party, the king of the scene,
But what lies beneath the surface, so rarely is seen.

He's a lady's man, a player, a heartbreaker,
But what he craves is real love, tired of being a faker.
He's got a reputation, a brand to maintain,
But all the while, he's searching for something to sustain.

He's a slave to desire, a pawn to his lust,
But deep down inside, he's just a man, not a must.

He's tired of the charade, the role he must play,
He longs for true love, a real meaningful say.

So don't be fooled by the myth of the playboy,
There's more to him than meets the eye, oh joy.
He's just a man, like you and me,
Searching for love and acceptance, endlessly.

44. THE WAY YOU MAKE ME FEEL

My love, you are a symphony
Of sensations, a wonder to behold
With each thrust, your melody
Rises and crests, a story untold

Your body is a canvas
And I am the brush
Stroking and painting
With each passionate rush
Your cream flows like a river
A sweet nectar to taste

I am addicted to your moans
Music to my ears
The taste of your love juice, better than lollipop
A drug that leaves me in a daze

Your orgasm is a fireworks show
A burst of colors in the night sky
I am the lucky observer
As you soar and reach new heights

My fingers are the conductor
Leading you to an orchestral crescendo
As you roll your eyes and moan
Your love spot is my heaven, a place I'll never let go.

45. THE ART OF SEDUCTION

The art of seduction is a delicate game
Of subtle glances and coy smiles, a flame
That flickers and dances, an alluring glow
A promise of pleasure, a taste of the unknown

It is the art of persuasion, a way to entice
To draw someone near and make them think twice
About the line they've drawn, the rules they've made
To make them question if they should be afraid

The art of seduction is a performance, a show
Of confidence and charm, a glint in the eye
It is the art of manipulation, to make them want more
To pull them in and make them feel alive

But beware, for seduction can be a dangerous game
It can lead to obsession, a never-ending flame
That consumes and destroys, a fire that never fades
So be careful who you play with, and the debts you make

For in the end, the art of seduction is a choice
A decision to follow your heart or use your voice
To say no, to walk away, to leave the dance
For in the end, it is you who holds the chance.

46. MY LATINA MUSE

My lovely Latina muse,
Thy beauty doth inspire,
Each night we spend together,
A passion doth transpire.

With legs spread wide,
Like a blooming flower,
You grant me access,
To your secret bower.

My pen in hand,
My dick in thee,
Together we craft,
Erotic poetry.
With every thrust,
And every word,
I am in awe,
Of thee, my bard.

Let us make magic,

Again tonight,
As you spread your legs,
And give me sight.
Of thy heavenly folds,
Like a treasure trove,
My inspiration, my Latina love.

47. SEX IN PARIS

Forget the music and the postcard view
That is not why I came out here with you
I did not come for art or pastry dough
Or places that the tourists like to go
I booked a room to see the iron tower
And celebrate the magic of the hour

I want you leaning on the metal bar
Beneath the glowing light of every star
The wind from off the river feels so cold
A lovely sight for me to just behold
I step behind to warm your cooling skin
And let the heavy action now begin

I cannot teach the language of the land
But I can take your tiny little hand
I am no poet with a book of verse
I only want to make you gasp and curse
You will not need a language anymore
As I begin to shake you to the core

This city is so famous for romance
But I am here to do a different dance

My version leaves a mark upon the skin
As we commit a very lovely sin
The tower pulses with a golden light
As we enjoy the middle of the night

I treat you like a royal queen right now
I wipe the sweat from off your pretty brow
But you are claimed completely by your king
Above the people and the noise they bring
Let tourists wander in the street below
They do not know the pleasure that we know

The tower fades into the dark of night
As I hold on to you with all my might
The only thing that matters is the pace
The look of pleasure on your pretty face
Paris is made for those who truly yearn
For those who want to watch the fire burn

48. DEMON MODE

Her face looks sweet and innocent to see
But that is not the way she is with me
Do not be fooled by looks that she might show
Because inside a fire starts to glow
At first she seemed a novice and so shy
But that was just a very clever lie

She slipped into a state of wild control
To take the body and the very soul
My body moved before my mind could think
She dragged me right unto the very brink

NATE HALIV: PLEASE EXCUSE ME FOR NOT BEING SHAKESPEARE

Her hips were rolling with a steady pace
A look of hunger was upon her face

Her tongue was moving with a perfect skill
To give my body such a heavy thrill
It felt like something from a holy book
With every single heavy breath she took
Delilah was not equal to this girl
She sent my senses in a messy whirl

She was not gentle or contained at all
She made the heavy barriers to fall
I tried to slow the rhythm down a bit
She would not stand for any part of it
She is a menace in the linen sheets
A goddess of the heavy rhythmic beats
I did not think belief was real or true
Until I saw exactly what you do
She pulled the sounds right out of my deep chest
She did not let me take a single rest
Her eyes rolled back into her pretty head
As we were playing in the messy bed

I stay right there and cannot look away
I want her chaos every single day
She is a queen of danger and of night
She makes the darkness feel extremely bright
Turn on the demon mode you hide so well
And put me back inside your magic spell

49. TILL WE MEET TO FUCK NO MORE

Until the day we meet and cannot touch
We hold the passion that we love so much
Our love is burning steady and so bright
To light the darkness of the heavy night
We will refuse to let the fire die
And keep the heat beneath the open sky

We lose ourselves inside the passion deep
A promise that we always mean to keep
The difference between us fades away
As we engage in all our lovers play
We feel the beating of a single heart
That nothing in the world can tear apart

Our bodies stay connected in the dark
To keep alive the very vital spark
We hold each other till the morning light
To end the pleasure of the lovely night
This love we have will never fade or die
It stays with us beneath the sunny sky

We savor every moment of the skin
And all the lovely trouble we are in
The heavy world will quickly fall away
Whenever we decide to start to play
This passion is not fragile or too weak
It is the only comfort that we seek

We stay together facing every fear
And keep our bodies very close and near
I choose you every time and every day

NATE HALIV: PLEASE EXCUSE ME FOR NOT BEING SHAKESPEARE

In every single kind of special way
Until the day we cannot do the deed
Our love will be the only thing we need

OTHER BOOKS BY NATE HALIV

- The Nigerian Prince
- The Girl Who Ran Without Legs
- Seeing the World Through a Black Woman's Eyes
- Lucy Far: The Untold Story of Child Trafficking
- A Letter to Feminists
- Heart Full of Pain

Made in the USA
Coppell, TX
05 February 2026

70243542R00049